...LE HARRY
...ND
...P OF DOOM

BY SUZY KLINE
Pictures by Frank Remkiewicz

SCHOLASTIC INC.
New York Toronto London Auckland Sydney
Mexico City New Delhi Hong Kong

ISBN 0-590-29068-1

Text copyright © 1998 by Suzy Kline. Illustrations copyright © 1998 by Frank Remkiewicz. All rights reserved. Published by Scholastic Inc., 555 Broadway, New York, NY 10012, by arrangement with Viking Children's Books, a division of Penguin Putnam Inc. SCHOLASTIC and associated logos are trademarks and/or registered trademarks of Scholastic Inc.

48 47 46 45 44 43 42 41 40 39 38   8 9/0

Printed in the U.S.A.   40

First Scholastic printing, September 1999

Set in New Century Schoolbook

Dedicated with love to my students:

Melissa Allison	Jonathon Hall
Michele Belanger	Daniel Hanusch
Lindsay Castaldi	Emily Homrok
Eric Collins	Iassic Languell
Kristine Dieckhoff	Jenna Matrascia
Christopher Doyle	Erin McBurney
Michael Dubreuil	Rebecca McKeen
Anthony Fieldman	Caitlin Mulherin
Stephanie Garrison	Nada Noujaim
Aaron Garves	Jared Pelchat
Matthew Gasparelli	Christopher Petit
Matthew Geraci	Joseph Roscello
Jonathan Gerardi	Erzsebet Sarkozi
Zachary Goulet	Michael Simmons
Francesco Graziano	Michael Stoecker

Catherine Trestini

And to my daughter Emily for the inspiration.
Thanks for a wonderful trip to Disney World.

Contents

The Red Envelope

Harry has been my best friend since kindergarten. He loves creepy things, slimy things, anything horrible.

Except . . . *one thing*.

And that's what Song Lee and I found out the last day of second grade. The *one horrible thing* Harry hates.

It all started with a red envelope.

"Look, Harry," I said as we walked

into class that morning. "There's something on our desks."

"Hey, Doug. It's a red envelope."

Harry and I ripped ours open.

"Hot dog!" Harry said. Then he made his eyebrows go up and down. "It's an invitation from Song Lee to an end-of-the-year party."

"I hope you can come," Song Lee said as she joined us. "I could only invite six people. Dad only had eight passes."

"Mountainside Park!" Ida exclaimed.

"Neato!" Harry and I said, slapping each other five.

"How did you get free passes?" Mary asked.

"My dad got them from work."

"Cool," Dexter said.

"I'm so excited!" Ida said, waving her

red invitation in the air. "I've never been to Mountainside Park. What's it like?"

"There's this one ride," I said, "Kasploosh Mountain, that is so great. You get in a canoe and go down a fifty-degree waterfall."

Harry rubbed his hands together. "Can't wait!"

"My favorite thing at amusement parks is the fun house," Ida said. "It's not scary like some rides."

"Main Street is cool," Dexter said. "It's right out of the fifties. They play rock-and-roll all day and all night. It'll be shoogie-boogie-boo time! I'm buying a big poster of Elvis."

"What's your favorite ride, Harry?" Song Lee asked.

Harry grinned. "The Haunted House."

"That's horrible!" Mary groaned. "You *would* like cobwebs in your face, ghosts, graveyards, and creepy noises!"

"They're the best!" Harry said, holding up two fingers for victory.

"I suppose you go on *all the rides*," Mary grumbled.

Harry flashed his white teeth. "All the scary ones."

Sidney tapped Harry on the shoulder. "Bet you haven't done the *newest ride.*"

"What newest ride?" we all asked.

"The one they just added at Mountainside Park," Sidney explained.

"I'll go on anything scary," Harry bragged.

"Is that a promise?" Sidney asked.

"Sure. What is it?"

Everyone gathered around as Sidney drew a picture of it in his notebook.

"It's this thirteen-story haunted hotel—"

"I love it already," Harry interrupted.

"Shhhh!" Mary scolded. She had to get her facts.

Sidney kept drawing. "And in this hotel is an elevator. You get in the elevator and go up to the thirteenth floor. Suddenly, SNAP! The cable breaks, and the elevator drops thirteen floors before it stops. The ride is called *The Drop of Doom*."

"Ooooooooooh," everyone replied.

"I'm *not* going on that," Mary said.

"Me either," Ida agreed.

Song Lee smiled. "I went with Father last weekend. It was so much fun! I go on it with you, Harry."

Harry's mouth looked like it had dropped thirteen floors! I could see his silver filling.

Dexter ran his fingers through his

hair. "Man, I'll have to check with Elvis on that one."

"It's a piece of cake. I've already done it," Sidney bragged. "My stepdad took me last weekend when it opened. Everyone shrieked and screamed bloody murder as we fell thirteen stories! And you know what?"

"What?" we all asked.

"We didn't die. We landed on the first floor just fine." Sidney pointed his pencil at Harry. "*You promised* to ride it."

Harry looked like he was going to throw up, but he managed to nod his head.

When the bell rang, and we all went back to our seats, Song Lee whispered to Harry, "Do you feel all right? You look sick."

Slowly, Harry turned and looked at us. His eyes were bulging.

"Promise you two won't tell?"

"Promise," I said.

Song Lee crossed her heart.

"I . . . *hate* . . . elevators. They give me the willies. I remember riding one in a department store, and it got stuck. The lights went out. It was dark. I screamed, I was so afraid!"

"How old were you?" Song Lee asked.

"Almost four."

"Man," I said. "That's a long time ago. You were practically a baby. You can do it now, Harry."

"Nope. I haven't gone on an elevator since. I always take the stairs. Now I have to do this ride and I don't know how I can."

Song Lee kneeled down next to

Harry. She put her chin on his desk. "I was afraid when I came to America. It was new school, new language. But . . . now, I'm happy. Sometimes you feel different about things *after you try them.*"

Harry shook his head. "I already tried an elevator. It gave me the heebie-jeebies!"

"But you were just a baby," she said. "You need to try one more time."

"I . . . *can't*," Harry groaned.

I stared at Harry. I couldn't believe it. This was a first! The one horrible thing Harry hated.

Elevators.

It looked like *The Drop of Doom* was going to be a nightmare for Harry!

The Present

After the pledge, I tried to cheer Harry up. "Look, the party is Friday. That's three days away. Forget *The Drop of Doom*. Think about . . . all the food we'll eat and drink. Think about those neat cobwebs and ghosts in the Haunted House. Think about . . ."

I looked at the teacher. "The surprise present we have for Miss Mackle!"

Harry suddenly sat up. "Her present!"

Harry's doom seemed to float away like a cloud. At least temporarily.

"Boys and girls," Miss Mackle said. "It's hard to believe that this is our last day of second grade. It's been such a wonderful year!"

When Song Lee took out her cherry blossom handkerchief, I knew she was going to cry.

No one wanted to leave Miss Mackle's class.

Mary raised her hand. "When will we find out who we have next year for third grade?"

Miss Mackle smiled. "Now."

Sidney leaned over. "Psssst, Harry! *I* want to know when you're going to ride *The Drop of Doom*. Is it going to be your first ride or last?"

Harry's fist froze with fear.

I answered for him. "Harry wants to save the best for last."

Sidney cackled. "I'll bet . . ."

Just then, Song Lee and Mary rushed to the front of the class. "First, we have gift for you, Miss Mackle," Song Lee said. "It is surprise."

"Song Lee's mother made it for us," Mary explained. "She came in one day when you were out. That's why you didn't know about it."

"My goodness," Miss Mackle said. "What a big box! What could this be?"

We all watched the teacher unfold the tissue paper and then hold up the five-foot-square quilt!

"It's beautiful!" Miss Mackle exclaimed.

"We each drew our own square. Mrs. Park sewed the squares together for us," Mary said.

"I bet I know who did this one," Miss Mackle said.

Everyone looked at the square with the green slime and ants and the snake costume.

"Harry!" everyone groaned.

Harry was frozen in thought.

Mary pointed to her square. "I did 'The Deadly Skit.' Remember?"

Miss Mackle replied. "I remember! There are the three dead kings and the angels and the piano player."

Mary beamed. She was the piano player.

"Do you like the kickball game?"

Dexter asked. "I did that one."

"Especially the soccer ball in the air!" Miss Mackle said. Then she looked closely at another square. "Is that you, Song Lee, as one of the dead fish?"

Song Lee nodded. "That's me and Harry."

I looked over at Harry. He looked like a dead fish now.

"Our Thanksgiving play!" Miss Mackle hugged the quilt. "I will treasure this, boys and girls. Thank you so much!"

We all clapped.

Then Mary popped the question again. "So who are we having next year for third grade?"

The class turned pin quiet.

Miss Mackle gently folded up her

quilt and placed it back in the box.

"Well, you will all be staying together and going to a new room on the second floor—Room 3B."

Sidney leaned back in his chair. "Too bad we can't take the elevator, huh, Harry?"

Harry gritted his teeth.

Mary doubled over like she had a bad stomach ache. "Another year with . . . Harry. Ooooooh," she groaned.

"Yup," Sidney chuckled. "Another year with ol' Harry the canary who thinks *The Drop of Doom* is too scary!"

Harry held up two fists. Now he was *mad*.

The rest of us waited to hear the name of our next year's teacher.

"And your teacher will be . . ."

I was disappointed she didn't reach for an envelope like on the Academy Awards.

". . . me."

No one said anything. It took a while to sink in.

Miss Mackle explained, "It's called *looping*. That's when the teacher moves to the next grade with her class."

The good news melted Harry's anger. He put his two fists down and flashed his white teeth. "All right!" he said.

Song Lee hugged Miss Mackle.

All of us cheered!

Except Mary. She plopped in her chair and folded her arms. "I have to be in Harry's room again? Puh-leeeeese say it isn't so!"

No one talked about *The Drop of Doom* any more until Friday.

Song Lee's House

Friday at noon, Harry and I walked slowly over to Song Lee's house.

"It's going to be a great end-of-the-year party," I said.

"Great party," Harry said.

"We're going to have fun."

"Fun."

"A cool time."

"A cool time," Harry repeated.

Suddenly, Harry stopped on the

stairs at Song Lee's house. "I'm out of here, Doug."

I grabbed the loop on Harry's jeans.

"Wait a minute! Do you want to miss the Haunted House?"

Harry shook his head.

"Do you want to miss Song Lee's party?"

Harry shook his head again.

"So, just don't do *that ride*."

I was careful not to say the E word.

Harry started walking up the steps again. "You're right. Everything else is going to be—"

"Howdy doody!" Sidney called as he skipped up the stairs behind us. "Ready-o to go?"

Harry rolled his eyes. "If it isn't Sid the Squid."

"And," Sidney replied, slapping Harry on the back, "Harry the Canary!

I wonder if you'll say 'Tweet, tweet!' when you fall like a bird for thirteen stories."

"Funny," Harry said. "Actually, I'm looking forward to the ride."

This was not going to be easy.

The three of us rang Song Lee's doorbell.

Mrs. Park answered. "Hello boys! We almost ready to hop in van. Come in!"

The first thing we noticed was the fifty-five-gallon aquarium in Song Lee's living room.

"Man, those goldfish are huge!" I said.

Harry and I went over and looked closely at their bright orange and yellow fins.

"They were pond goldfish," Song Lee said. "They get very big. I name them Chong and Chang."

"Hi, Chong," I said.

"Hi, Chang," Harry said.

Sidney came over and looked at the huge sand castle in the middle of the tank. "Hey, that has about thirteen floors, too."

Harry cringed.

"Okay boys and girls," Mrs. Park said. "Everyone here. Hop in van and go to Mountainside Park."

Everyone scooted into the back of the car. Song Lee sat next to Harry.

When we were on the highway, she talked to him very softly.

"Don't worry about *Drop of Doom*. There are lots of other rides that are fun."

"But . . . I have to do it. Sidney will be on my case all next year in third grade."

"It is that important to you?"

"Yes."

"Then I will help you, Harry. I know when drop comes. You can squeeze my hand and close your eyes. Remember *Alice in Wonderland*?"

"Yeah." Harry smiled. "I love that story."

"Well, it's like Alice falling down that hole. You may be surprised and even like it."

Harry nodded. I think talking about it helped.

"Remember when I didn't want to be in our Thanksgiving play," Song Lee said. "I was afraid to speak. You thought up part for me without words."

"A dead fish." Harry laughed. "You were great."

"Well, now I help you ride that *elevator.*"

Harry shivered.

Song Lee had said it.

The E word.

Thirty minutes later we drove under the wooden arch that said MOUNTAINSIDE PARK. There were signs everywhere! Sidney was the first to point out the big billboard about the new ride.

It was a scary picture of a haunted hotel with an elevator dangling on the edge by one *thin* cord.

"THE DROP OF DOOM!" everyone shouted.

When I looked at Harry's arm, I could see goose pimples.

Mountainside Park

"*Be bop de boo,*
Be bop de boo,
Shoogey boogie
Boogie shoogey
Be bop de boo,"

Dexter sang as we walked down Main
Street in Mountainside Park.

"Look at that car parked over there!"
I said. "It's a 1955 Buick. Man, I love

the fins in the back. Neato, huh, Harry?"

"Listen to Elvis," Dexter said, pointing to a speaker next to a streetlight. "He's singing 'Jailhouse Rock.' "

Mrs. Park carried her picnic basket and cooler over to a shaded table.

"Time for lunch. We eat now."

Everyone watched Song Lee's mother as she spread out a butterfly tablecloth and paper plates. "We have cold chicken, egg sandwich, potato salad, and three Korean dish, *pulgogi*—that is

beef strip, *kalbi*—short rib, and *kim-chi*—cabbage and vegetable!"

Sidney grabbed a chicken leg. "Good grub."

While Mrs. Park poured everyone ice tea, I tried the kimchi. "This is delicious," I said. "There are peppers and cucumbers in it too."

"It is traditional Korean dish," Song Lee said, reaching for the soy sauce.

Ida and Mary nodded. "We had some before at your house. It's our favorite."

Song Lee served some kimchi to Harry.

But he just picked at it. He wasn't hungry.

"I buy everyone ice cream later for dessert," Mrs. Park said.

The first ride we went on was Kasploosh. It was in a fake mountain with canals going up and down and around. The last part of the ride was a fifty-foot waterfall.

"How long is the wait?" Sidney groaned. Then he looked at Harry. "I can't wait to go on *The Drop of Doom.*"

"Twenty minute," Mrs. Park said. "Maybe Dexter sing us Elvis tune."

"Sure!" Dexter said as he pretended to strum a guitar and sing.

Song Lee took Harry's hands and started to rock-and-roll right there in line. It was a good distraction. Harry always loved to dance.

Mary and Ida danced too.

When Sidney asked me to dance, I said, "Forget it."

Finally, we got to the top of the fake mountain.

The attendant helped six of us climb into the wide canoe. Mrs. Park went with Sidney in the canoe behind us.

"Here we go!" I said. "This is my favorite ride."

We chugged down the river, dipped in a cave, and then went around a mountainside. It was neat seeing all the people walk around below.

When we came to the waterfall, I put my hands up.

"Here come the falls!"

Harry put his hands up. So did Song Lee.

"WHEEEEEEEEEEEEEEEE!"

Our canoe plunged down the water-fall! Water sprayed in our face.

Sidney screamed. Mary closed her eyes as her braids flew in the air.

Song Lee, Harry, and I called out,
"YEEEEEEEHAW!"

Kasplooooooooooooooooosh!

"That was so much fun!" I said when we finally hit the bottom of the river and coasted to the gate.

"I'm not going on that again," Mary said. "I got all wet."

"Party pooper," Sidney said.

"You should talk!" Mary scolded. "You screamed louder than anyone else, Sidney La Fleur."

Harry made a wide smile. He was gaining courage. "I love Kasploosh," he said.

"You love the rides at Mountainside, Harry," I said.

Then he glanced over at the haunted hotel. "Let's . . . do the Haunted House next," he said.

The Haunted House

The line wasn't so bad at the Haunted House.

It only took us ten minutes.

Song Lee and Mary and Harry and I got into one car. We weren't happy about the girls getting the front seat.

Dexter and Sidney and Ida and Mrs. Park rode in the car behind us. We could see them because our cars were just a few yards apart.

"I think I'm feeling better about things," Harry whispered to Song Lee. "I think I can do that ride."

I noticed he didn't say the E word.

"You can do it, Harry," Song Lee replied as she turned around and smiled.

As soon as our cars passed the first set of doors, it got pitch black.

"AAAAAAAUUUUUUUGH!" Mary screamed. "What was that?"

"Just cobwebs," Harry laughed.

I noticed the little girl in the car in front of us was leaning over. She was trying to touch something.

When we came to a cemetery, I pointed to the tombstones.

"These epitaphs are funny," I said.

"I'll read some:

"*Here lie the bones of Oliver Bright*
He turned left
When he shoulda turned right.

"*Here lies Henry Horace McCall*
Hit in the head
By a cannonball."

As our cars moved along the track inside the dark haunted house, Sidney made up his own epitaph. He cupped his hands and shouted:

"*Here lies Harry*
No more in this room.
He didn't survive
The Drop of Doom."

Harry ground his fist in his hand. A moment later, a ghost popped out of a tombstone and said, *"Whoooooo are yoooouuuu?"*

"AAAAAAAAAUUUUUUGH!" Sidney screamed.

Suddenly our ride stopped.

No one moved.

Mrs. Lee called out, "Everyone calm?"

Sidney scrunched down in the car, moaning, *"That ghost is going to get us."*

Harry froze.

We were stuck in the dark.

Song Lee and I knew what Harry was thinking. This had happened before when he was three and a half!

Only it was in an elevator.

Mary looked around. "Something broke down. It looks like we're stuck in here."

Mrs. Park put her arm around Ida. *"Everyone calm!"* she called.

Harry buried his head in my lap.

"Harry!" Mary exclaimed as she turned around. "I don't believe it!"

When she talked, her white teeth glowed in the dark.

"Look!" Sidney shivered. *"Floating teeth!"*

"Cool," Dexter said.

"We'll get out of here," Mary said. "Sometimes these things happen. It did to my uncle when he was on the Octopus."

Mrs. Park counted heads. "Everyone safe and sound."

Suddenly, the ride started up again!

Mary looked at her glow-in-the-dark watch. "Two minutes, ten seconds. That wasn't too bad."

As our cars passed through the last door and into bright daylight again, everyone sighed. *"Phew!"*

The attendant was talking to that little girl. "Don't ever get out of the car," he said gently. "That makes the whole ride stop."

The little girl was crying. "I'm sorry. I just wanted to touch the ghost."

As we walked outside in the hot June sun, Mrs. Park suggested, "How about ice cream break?"

"Yeah," Sidney said. "I bet Harry gets lemon sherbet. People who are yellow love that flavor. Did you see him hide in Doug's lap?"

Everyone looked at Harry.

"I *was* afraid," he confessed.

"I don't believe it," Mary said. "You actually admitted it."

"Ol' Yeller," Sidney chuckled.

Mary scowled. "You know, Sidney, I like Harry better now. And *you* less!"

Sidney took a step back.

"It wasn't as bad as I thought it would be," Harry said. "I . . . *think* I'm ready for *that ride* now."

Song Lee jumped up and down.

Mary held up her hand. "Slap me five, Harry. I am too."

"I guess I'll go. I don't want to be left behind," Ida said.

We all got ice cream and licked it slowly as we walked over to . . .

THE DROP OF DOOM.

The Drop of Doom

"This is the best party I've ever been to," Mary said as we stood in the long line at The Drop of Doom licking our ice cream.

"It is Song Lee's idea," Mrs. Park said.

Song Lee beamed. "I love scary rides."

Dexter unfolded his poster of Elvis. "Do you think Miss Mackle would hang this in our third grade classroom?"

"Forget it, Dex," Mary moaned.

"I could sure go for another chicken leg," Sidney said. Then he pretended to bite Harry's knee.

"Funny," Harry snapped.

As our line wound around the garden of the haunted hotel, we could hear the screams of people inside the elevator as they went down.

"Did you see that?" Ida said. "The doors opened on the thirteenth floor and the people could see out over the park."

Sidney started to shake. "They can?"

"Hey, I thought you said you rode this ride?" Mary said.

"I did."

"Watch," Ida said, pointing to the thirteenth floor. "It's going to happen again when the next ride starts."

We waited.

I thought the lightning bolts stuck on the roof were neat.

Suddenly the doors of the elevator opened. We could see the people sitting there waiting to drop.

Then the doors closed and the elevator dropped thirteen floors. "*Aaaaaaaauuuuuugh!*" the people shrieked as they fell to the bottom floor.

"I like the part when the doors open," Harry said. "It's the *closed elevator* part that I don't like."

There.

Harry said it in front of everybody.

Mary replied first. "So elevators scare you?"

"Yup."

"I can't do merry-go-rounds. They make me dizzy." Then Mary added, "You know something, Harry? I'm not so bugged anymore that you're in my third grade class."

Harry smiled. Then he showed her a red salamander he had found in the garden.

"AAAAAUUUUUUUUUGH!" Mary screamed.

Ten minutes later we entered the hotel. There were lots of cobwebs and portraits of weird people up on the walls. A butler in a black tux with a low voice greeted us.

"Welcome to the haunted hotel. You are invited to the thirteenth floor . . . by *elevator.*"

Mary turned to Song Lee. "How long is the ride?"

"About three minutes."

"How long is the . . . *fall*?"

"Seconds," Song Lee said.

Mary looked at Ida. "We can do it."

Harry stepped closer to Song Lee.

As we passed a counter on the left, I could see people buying souvenirs. There were T-shirts that said I SURVIVED THE DROP OF DOOM!

And some people were buying pictures.

"What are the pictures of?" I asked.

"There's a camera hidden in the elevator. It takes a picture when the elevator doors open," Mary explained. "It says so on that sign."

"I buy one," Mrs. Park said. "We see how we look!"

Song Lee giggled when the people in the next car shrieked going down.

We moved to the front of the line.

"It's *your turn*," the butler said in his creepy low voice. "We hope you return."

Mary and Ida held hands.

Dexter put on his dark glasses.

I SURVIVED
the
DROP
of
DOOM

"Elvis would wear these on the ride."

"Cool," I said.

Dexter ran his fingers through his hair. "I'm going to be real cool when those doors fly open on the thirteenth floor."

Sidney got a ghostly look when

Dexter said that.

"Puh-leeeeeeese enter here," the butler said.

"I can do this," Mary said.

"Harry can too." Song Lee smiled.

"You'd make a good coach, Song Lee," I said.

Creeak! The two sliding doors opened.

There it was.

The elevator.

There were exactly eight seats!

We all sat down and put on our seat belts.

Then we lowered the steel bar over our laps.

Harry sat between Song Lee and me. Sidney was in the back row.

"Well, Song Lee," Harry whispered. "I wouldn't be on this elevator *without you*."

"We help each other," she replied.

Blam!

The elevator doors closed.

Slowly we chugged up, up, up to each new floor. Harry held tight to the seat bar. "Let me know when we're going to fall."

"Not yet," Song Lee whispered.

Up, up, up. Harry counted the floors. This was the seventh . . .

eighth . . .

ninth . . .

tenth . . .

eleventh . . .

twelfth . . .

"Get ready," Song Lee whispered. "The doors are going to open on the next floor."

Swoooooooosh!

As the doors opened, we could feel a nice breeze and hear the music from the merry-go-round.

Harry looked out at Mountainside Park. "Neato! There's Kasploosh

Mountain!" he said. "And the Haunted House."

"I see Main Street," Dexter said.

"Now!" Song Lee said.

Harry grabbed Song Lee's hand.

"AAAAUUUU
      UUUUUUUUU
      UUUUUUUU
      UUUUUUU
         AAAAUUUUUGH!"

Thirteen floors of *free fall!*

Everyone in the car screamed as the elevator fell down,
                    down,
                       down,
                          down!

"It's Wonderland!" Harry shouted. "I feel like a feather, I don't weigh anything!"

"Aaaaaaaahhhhhhhhh!"

The last few floors felt like we were bouncing on a trampoline.

Phooooooomf! We landed!

"Cool!" Dexter said, whipping off his dark glasses.

"You did it, Harry!" Song Lee said.

Harry had his biggest smile ever in second grade. "I *really did* do it! You were right, Song Lee . . . it *was* like falling down a hole."

Sidney popped out of his seat. "I loved it! Enjoyed every minute of it!"

As we walked by the picture counter, Mrs. Park purchased one T-shirt and the shot of our elevator.

When we saw our faces we laughed.

Especially Sidney's.

His eyes were closed!

"No wonder you don't remember that door flying open," I said. "You had your

Memories of Mountainside Park

eyes closed the whole time, Sid. You're one cool dude!"

Sidney made a face. "At least I wasn't afraid to go on it, like Harry!"

Harry nodded. "You're right, Sid. I was. But you know what? Thanks to

Song Lee, I can go on any elevator now! It's the greatest feeling *not to be afraid.*"

Song Lee clapped her hands.

"So who wants to go with me a second time?" Harry asked.

"Me!" Song Lee said.

"Me!" the rest of us shouted, running back into the line.

Mrs. Park plopped down on the cooler and waited for us at the bottom of the haunted hotel. She looked kind of beat in her souvenir shirt.